BAKIN' BROWNIES

12 delicious recipes for
brownies, blondies, and bars

BY SUSAN DEVINS

ILLUSTRATED BY YVONNE CATHCART

DUTTON CHILDREN'S BOOKS
NEW YORK

Contents

Brownie Bonanza

Chewy, gooey, cakey, flaky—any way you cook them, brownies are yummy!

Almost every family has a favorite brownie recipe in its cooking inventory. Just ask your mom, dad, aunt, uncle, or grandparent to describe their most cherished brownie recipe from childhood.

Each recipe has its own special character. Fruits, nuts, marshmallows, oats, chocolate chips, coconut, caramel, white chocolate, mint chocolate, milk chocolate, or bittersweet chocolate can be added to the mixture. The only limit is your imagination.

Baking brownies, blondies, and bars is so easy, using the ingredients that most cooks have in their kitchen. They require only a few minutes to put together and most are ready to eat in less than half an hour.

Always keep brownies, blondies, and bars on hand. Cut them into squares, store them at room temperature, or freeze them (if they last that long) and have them available all year round.

So get ready to have fun bakin' brownies, blondies, and bars!

What do great bakers earn?

—Brownie points

Batter Up: Baking Basics

1. Read the entire recipe and make sure you have all the ingredients.

2. Assemble your equipment.

3. Assemble your ingredients, including those that are chopped or melted.

4. Adjust the oven rack to the middle, and preheat the oven to the necessary temperature.

5. Grease the *Bakin' Brownies* pan. Vegetable spray makes the task easy! You can also use butter.

6. Measure the dry ingredients by spooning lightly into the dry-ingredient measuring cup until overflowing. Don't shake the cup! Level off with a straight knife or spatula. Use the same technique to measure baking powder, baking soda, salt, and spices into measuring spoons, by dipping and filling the spoons and then leveling off with a spatula. To measure brown sugar, pack it firmly into the cup and level it with a spatula. Use a wire whisk to mix the dry ingredients together in a bowl.

7. Measure the liquid ingredients in a spouted clear glass or plastic measuring cup by pouring to the correct measuring point clearly marked on the outside of the cup. Then bend down to check the measurement at eye level.

8. To measure sticks of butter, use the measurement marks on the wrapper as a guide. If there are no markings, remember that one stick of butter (in a package of four) equals 8 tablespoons (125 mL).

9. In most brownie recipes, both the butter and chocolate are used melted. They should be melted in a saucepan over very low heat.

10. Whisk the cooled melted butter and chocolate in a large mixing bowl. Then beat in the sugar, eggs, and flavoring. At this point the batter might look grainy, but that's okay.

11. To combine liquid and dry ingredients, add the flour mixture to the beaten egg mixture and blend it with a spoon or whisk until the particles of flour have been absorbed. Try not to overbeat the batter.

12. Pour the batter into the prepared pan. Scrape the bottom and sides of the bowl with a rubber spatula as you pour. Gently spread the batter to the edges of the pan in an even layer.

13. Wear oven mitts or use pot holders when putting the brownie pan into the oven.

COOK'S DEFINITIONS

Beat: Combine ingredients rapidly with a spoon, a fork, or an electric mixer, using a circular stirring motion. This adds air to the batter, producing a smooth mixture.

Mix: Stir ingredients evenly with a spoon, a whisk, or a fork.

Combine: Blend sets of ingredients together.

Fold: Using a rubber spatula, mix gently by cutting down in the center and lifting toward the edge of the bowl.

Sift: Pass dry ingredients like flour, salt, baking powder, or baking soda through a fine-meshed strainer to remove lumps and lighten texture.

5

14. Brownies are baked when the top is set. Check to see if they are done by inserting a toothpick into the center of the batter. If it comes out with only a few moist crumbs sticking to it, the brownies are done.

15. Remove the brownie pan and transfer to a wire rack. Let the brownies, blondies, or bars cool thoroughly before slicing. It's okay if brownies sag slightly or the top cracks a bit.

16. Eat the brownies, blondies, or bars and share them with your friends. Bet you can't eat just one!

Cook's Safety Tips

1. Always wash your hands and wipe the counters clean before beginning.

2. Wear an apron and use oven mitts or pot holders.

3. Always have an adult nearby to help, especially when you're using the oven.

4. If you burn yourself, run cold water on the burn right away and call for help.

5. Ask an adult for help with chopping, and always use a cutting board.

6. Remember to turn off the oven when finished.

7. Clean up the kitchen as you go along. Put ingredients away as you use them; wash, dry, and put away all utensils; be sure to dry metal baking pans thoroughly to prevent rusting; wipe counters and tables.

Cook's Tools

- *Bakin' Brownies* pan

- mixing bowls

- measuring cups for dry ingredients

- measuring cups for liquid ingredients (clear glass or plastic)

- measuring spoons

- chopping board and safe knife for dicing fruits or nuts or marshmallows

- wire whisk

- large wooden spoon and rubber spatula

- fork, knife

- grater, peeler

- small, medium, and large saucepans

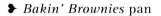

- electric mixer

- wire rack for cooling

How are brownies like a baseball team?

—They need a good batter.

7

The Very Best Brownies

What you need:

2 ounces (56 g) unsweetened chocolate

1/2 cup (125 mL) unsalted butter

2 eggs

1 cup (250 mL) sugar

1 teaspoon (5 mL) vanilla

1/2 cup (125 mL) flour

pinch of salt

What you do:

1. Preheat oven to 350°F (180°C) and grease the brownie pan.

2. In a small saucepan over low heat, carefully melt chocolate and butter. Remove from heat to cool.

3. In a large bowl, beat eggs and sugar until thick. Add vanilla. Fold chocolate mixture into egg and sugar mixture. Mix thoroughly.

4. Sift flour and salt in a separate bowl and then fold gently into the batter, mixing until just blended.

5. Pour batter into the prepared pan. Bake for 20 minutes or until a toothpick inserted in the center comes out with a few moist crumbs still attached.

6. Transfer pan to wire rack to cool completely before cutting the brownies into squares.

COOKING CLUES

- To check for doneness of brownies, you can use an uncooked piece of spaghetti instead of a toothpick.

- Break eggs into a cup first, then add to other ingredients. This prevents the shell from getting into the batter.

- Store marshmallows in the freezer to keep them fresh and prevent them from drying out.

- To get the most juice out of a lemon: Press down on the fruit with both hands, roll it several times back and forth over a hard surface, and then cut it in half. Squeezing out the juice will be easy.

- To soften hard brown sugar, put sugar and a slice of soft bread in an airtight container. Within a few hours the sugar will absorb the bread's moisture and soften.

Ooey-Gooey Marshmallow Brownies

What you need:

2 ounces (56 g) unsweetened chocolate

1/2 cup (125 mL) semisweet chocolate chips

1/2 cup (125 mL) unsalted butter

2 eggs

1 cup (250 mL) sugar

1 teaspoon (5 mL) vanilla

1/2 cup (125 mL) flour

1/4 teaspoon (1 mL) salt

1/2 teaspoon (2 mL) baking powder

1 cup (250 mL) mini-marshmallows

Why did the thief rob a dessert table?

—He heard the brownies were rich.

What you do:

1. Preheat oven to 350°F (180°C) and grease the brownie pan.

2. Melt unsweetened chocolate, chocolate chips, and butter in a saucepan on very low heat. Stir together and cool slightly.

3. Beat together eggs, sugar, and vanilla in a large bowl.

4. Beat in chocolate mixture.

5. Mix flour, salt, and baking powder in a separate bowl. Stir into chocolate mixture until just blended. Stir in mini-marshmallows.

6. Spread batter evenly in pan. Bake for 30 minutes.

7. Transfer pan to wire rack and cool completely before cutting the brownies into squares.

BROWNIE POINTS
Clever new ways to cut brownies, blondies, or bars:

Triangles: Cut the brownies into squares and halve each one diagonally.

Diamonds: Make straight parallel cuts 1 1/2 inches apart down the length of the pan, then make diagonal cuts about 1 1/2 inches apart across the width of the pan, keeping the lines even.

Rectangles: Make long narrow rectangles, and serve them with a mound of ice cream.

11

Super Extrafudgy Brownies

What you need:

3 ounces (84 g) bittersweet chocolate, chopped

1 ounce (28 g) unsweetened chocolate, chopped

6 tablespoons (90 mL) unsalted butter

3/4 cup (175 mL) sugar

1 teaspoon (5 mL) vanilla

2 eggs

1/2 teaspoon (2 mL) salt

1/2 cup (125 mL) flour

1/4 cup (50 mL) semisweet chocolate chips

BROWNIE POINTS

**To store baked brownies: Once the
cooled brownies are cut, layer them
in a metal cookie tin, separating the
layers with sheets of waxed paper.
They keep nicely in an airtight
container at room temperature for
several weeks.**

What you do:

1. Preheat oven to 350°F (180°C) and grease the brownie pan.

2. In a heavy saucepan, melt bittersweet and unsweetened chocolate and butter over low heat, stirring until smooth. Remove pan from heat. Transfer mixture to a large bowl and cool until lukewarm.

3. Whisk in sugar and vanilla. Add eggs, one at a time, whisking well until the mixture is smooth. Stir in salt and flour until just combined; then stir in chocolate chips.

4. Spread batter evenly in pan. Bake for 22 minutes, or until a toothpick inserted in the center comes out with only a few crumbs sticking to it.

5. Transfer pan to wire rack and cool completely before cutting the brownies into squares.

Black-and-White Snowflake Brownies

What you need:

3 ounces (84 g) unsweetened chocolate

6 tablespoons (90 mL) unsalted butter

1 cup (250 mL) sugar

1/4 teaspoon (1 mL) baking powder

1/4 teaspoon (1 mL) salt

2 eggs

1 teaspoon (5 mL) vanilla

1/2 cup (125 mL) flour

1/2 cup (125 mL) white chocolate chips

What you do:

1. Preheat oven to 350°F (180°C) and grease the brownie pan.

2. In a small saucepan over low heat, melt chocolate and butter until smooth. Transfer mixture to a medium bowl and allow to cool slightly.

3. Stir in sugar, baking powder, salt, eggs, and vanilla. Beat well.

4. Stir in flour a little bit at a time until just blended.

5. Stir in white chocolate chips.

6. Spread batter evenly in pan. Bake for 25 minutes, or until a toothpick inserted in the center comes out with a few moist crumbs still attached.

7. Transfer pan to wire rack to cool completely before cutting the brownies into squares.

Why can't you tease egg whites?

—They can't take a yoke.

15

Cool-As-a-Breeze Mint Chocolate Chip Brownies

What you need:

1/2 cup (125 mL) unsalted butter, cut into pieces

2 ounces (56 g) unsweetened chocolate, chopped

1 cup (250 mL) mint chocolate chips

1 cup (250 mL) sugar

1/2 teaspoon (2 mL) vanilla

2 eggs

2/3 cup (150 mL) flour

1/2 teaspoon (2 mL) salt

What you do:

1. Preheat oven to 350°F (180°C) and grease the brownie pan.

2. In medium saucepan over low heat, melt butter, unsweetened chocolate, and 1/2 cup mint chocolate chips, stirring until smooth. Remove pan from heat, transfer mixture to a large bowl, and cool for ten minutes before stirring in sugar and vanilla.

3. Add eggs, one at a time, beating with a wooden spoon until the mixture is glossy and smooth.

4. Stir in flour, salt, and remaining mint chocolate chips until just combined.

mint

5. Spread batter evenly in pan and bake for 28-30 minutes.

6. Transfer pan to wire rack and cool completely before cutting the brownies into squares.

BROWNIE FOLKLORE

- Some people believe that the first brownie was an Australian sweet bread made in 1883 with brown sugar and currants.

- Culinary folklorists say the origin of the brownie is told in the story of a cook whose chocolate cake did not rise nearly enough on baking. Not wanting to waste the dessert, the cook cut the solid piece into small squares and served it anyway.

- The earliest recipe, according to cookbook author and dessert authority Maida Heatter, was for Bangor Brownies. It originally appeared in a cookbook published by the local YWCA in 1914, according to Mrs. "Brownie" Schrumpf, a member of the Maine Historical Society.

Bubbly Butterscotch-Toffee Blondies

What you need:

3/4 cup (175 mL) flour

1 teaspoon (5 mL) baking powder

pinch of salt

1/4 cup (50 mL) unsalted butter

1/2 cup (125 mL) sugar

1/2 cup (125 mL) light brown sugar

1 egg, slightly beaten

1 teaspoon (5 mL) vanilla

3/4 cup (175 mL) finely chopped Skor® candy bars or other chocolate-covered toffee bits

BROWNIE POINTS

After the brownies, blondies, or bars are baked, cut them into different shapes with cookie cutters. Place two on a dessert plate, overlapping. Put four strawberries or raspberries and some sliced kiwi on the plate, then drizzle chocolate syrup in a swirl design on top. Sprinkle with confectioners' sugar. Your guests will be very impressed!

18

What you do:

1. Preheat oven to 350°F (180°C) and grease the brownie pan.

2. In a medium bowl, combine flour, baking powder, and salt.

3. In a medium-size saucepan, melt butter; then transfer to a large bowl. Stir in sugar and brown sugar until well blended. Allow to cool before stirring in the egg and vanilla.

4. Stir the flour mixture into the butter mixture until just blended; then add the toffee bits.

5. Scrape the batter into the pan and spread evenly. Bake until blondies just begin to pull away from the sides of the pan, about 28-30 minutes.

6. Transfer pan to wire rack to cool completely before cutting the blondies into squares.

Dot-to-Dot Chocolate Blondies

What you need:

6 tablespoons (90 mL) unsalted butter

1 cup (250 mL) brown sugar

1 egg

1 teaspoon (5 mL) vanilla

1 cup (250 mL) flour

1 teaspoon (5 mL) baking powder

1/4 teaspoon (1 mL) salt

1/2 cup (125 mL) semisweet chocolate chips

What you do:

1. Preheat oven to 350°F (180°C) and grease the brownie pan.

2. In a heavy, large saucepan over low heat, melt the butter. Using a wooden spoon, stir in sugar and heat until the mixture begins to boil around the edges. Remove from heat, transfer the mixture to a large bowl, and cool for 5 minutes.

3. With a fork, beat egg and vanilla into butter mixture until blended.

4. Add flour, baking powder, and salt, mixing with a rubber spatula until just blended. Stir in chocolate chips.

5. Scrape the batter into the pan and spread evenly. Bake for 20-22 minutes.

6. Transfer pan to wire rack to cool completely before cutting the blondies into squares.

vanilla flower

Nifty Coconut-Nut Bars

What you need:

Bottom layer: 1/2 cup (125 mL) unsalted butter

1/4 (50 mL) cup sugar

5 tablespoons (75 mL) unsweetened cocoa

1 egg

1/2 teaspoon (2 mL) vanilla

1 3/4 cups (425 mL) graham cracker crumbs

1 cup (250 mL) shredded coconut

1/4 cup (50 mL) chopped walnuts

Middle layer: 1/2 cup (125 mL) unsalted butter

2 cups (250 mL) confectioners' sugar

2 tablespoons (25 mL) vanilla custard powder

3 tablespoons (45 mL) light cream

Top layer: 4 ounces (112 g) semisweet chocolate

2 tablespoons (25 mL) butter

What you do:

1. For bottom layer, grease the brownie pan.

2. Melt 1/2 cup butter, sugar, cocoa, egg, and vanilla in heavy saucepan over low heat, stirring until mixture reaches a custardlike consistency. Remove from heat, transfer mixture to large bowl, and stir in graham cracker crumbs, coconut, and walnuts. Mix well and pat down into brownie pan. Chill for 15 minutes.

3. For middle layer, cream 1/2 cup butter, confectioners' sugar, vanilla custard powder, and light cream. Beat until creamy and spread over bottom layer. Chill for 15 minutes.

4. For top layer, melt chocolate and butter in a saucepan over low heat, stir together until smooth, cool slightly, and pour over middle layer. Refrigerate for 1 to 2 hours until totally hard, then cut the bars into squares.

BROWNIE POINTS

Recycle leftover brownies by breaking them into bits and mixing them into vanilla ice cream to make your own brownie sundae!

Twice-As-Nice Rice Krispies® Bars

What you need:

1/3 cup (75 mL) unsalted butter

3 cups (750 mL) mini-marshmallows

1/4 teaspoon (1 mL) vanilla

4 cups (1 L) Rice Krispies® cereal

BROWNIE POINTS

Make a brownie gift basket (great for birthday presents and teacher presents). Cover gift boxes, inside and out, with pretty wrapping paper. New shoe boxes, stationery boxes, candy containers, and so forth, make great choices. Line the inside with waxed paper and stack the brownies in separate layers.

What you do:

1. Very lightly grease the brownie pan.

2. In a large saucepan over low heat, melt the butter. Add marshmallows, stirring until melted. Remove from heat.

3. Stir in vanilla. Add cereal, stirring until coated. (As a bonus you could add chocolate chips or your favorite nuts, too!)

4. Using a spatula, press into pan. Cool. Cut into squares.

Lightly Lemon Bars

What you need:

Crust: 1/2 cup (125 mL) butter, at room temperature
1/4 cup (50 mL) confectioners' sugar
1 cup (250 mL) flour
1/4 teaspoon (1 mL) salt

Filling: 2 eggs, beaten
1 cup (250 mL) sugar
2 tablespoons (25 mL) flour
1/2 teaspoon (2 mL) baking powder
4 tablespoons (60 mL) lemon juice
grated rind of 1/2 lemon
confectioners' sugar (to sprinkle on top)

What you do:

1. Preheat oven to 350°F (180°C) and lightly grease the brownie pan.

2. Make crust by beating together butter, confectioners' sugar, flour, and salt until blended. Pat into greased pan. Bake 15-20 minutes or until the pastry is light brown. Take it out of oven.

3. Make filling by beating together eggs, sugar, flour, baking powder, lemon juice, and lemon rind. Pour the mixture over the cooked crust.

4. Bake for 25 minutes or until set.

5. Transfer pan to wire rack and cool bars completely before cutting into squares. Sift confectioners' sugar over the bars.

Surprise-Your-Parents-with-Coffee-Cake Bars

What you need:

Filling: 1/4 cup (50 mL) sugar

2 tablespoons (25 mL) cinnamon

3 tablespoons (45 mL) semisweet chocolate chips

Batter: 1 cup (250 mL) sour cream

1 teaspoon (5 mL) baking soda

1/2 cup (125 mL) unsalted, softened butter

1 cup (250 mL) sugar

2 eggs

1 1/2 cups (375 mL) flour

1 1/2 teaspoons (7 mL) baking powder

1 teaspoon (5 mL) vanilla

What you do:

1. Preheat oven to 350°F (180°C) and grease the brownie pan.

2. Combine the filling ingredients (sugar, cinnamon, and chocolate chips). Set aside 3 tablespoons of the mixture to sprinkle on top of the bars before baking.

3. In a small bowl, mix sour cream with baking soda and set aside.

4. In a large bowl, cream butter and sugar together using an electric mixer. When the mixture is smooth, add the eggs. Add the sour cream mixture to the creamed butter, sugar, and eggs.

5. Add flour, baking powder, and vanilla to the creamed mixture.

6. Pour half the batter into the pan and layer with the sugar-cinnamon-chocolate chips mixture. Pour remaining batter over this. Top with the 3 tablespoons of filling mixture that was set aside.

7. Bake for 46-48 minutes. Transfer pan to wire rack and cool bars before cutting into squares.

Up-to-Date Bars

What you need:

1/3 cup (75 mL) unsalted, softened butter

1 cup (250 mL) brown sugar

1 egg

1 teaspoon (5 mL) vanilla

1 cup (250 mL) flour

1/4 teaspoon (1 mL) baking soda

1/2 teaspoon (2 mL) baking powder

1/2 teaspoon (2 mL) salt

1/4 cup (50 mL) semisweet chocolate chips

1/2 cup (125 mL) chopped dates

What you do:

1. Preheat oven to 350°F (180°C) and lightly grease the brownie pan.

2. In the large bowl of an electric mixer, cream together butter and sugar until light and fluffy. Beat in egg and vanilla.

3. In a separate bowl, sift together flour, baking soda, baking powder, and salt and add to egg mixture. Beat until well combined.

4. Add chocolate chips and dates.

5. Pour the batter into pan and spread evenly. Bake for 28 minutes.

6. Transfer pan to wire rack and cool completely before cutting the bars into squares.

THE SCIENCE OF BAKING

Isn't it amazing that combining and cooking the raw ingredients flour, butter, sugar, eggs, vanilla, baking powder, and chocolate can result in delicious, delectable brownies, blondies, and bars?

Baking is a science and the kitchen is your laboratory. You have to mix your ingredients properly to get the best results.

Leaveners, such as baking powder or baking soda, cause the batter to rise by producing carbon dioxide (a gas), which moves through the batter and gives it a light texture. The heat of the oven also contributes to the rising of the brownie, blondie, or bar as the gases in the batter expand. The egg also contributes to the volume by incorporating air — that is why angel cakes, which are made mostly of whipped egg, are so tall. The protein in the egg "coagulates" or forms a solid network, which, together with the protein in the flour, provides the structure for the brownies. The sugar competes with the protein in the flour for the water and contributes to the tenderness of the brownies, as well as the flavor. The butter traps the air that was whipped into the batter during mixing and makes the texture of the brownies soft. The surface of the brownies begins to firm up and brown, and in less than thirty minutes, you have a delicious treat!

31

To JJ, my Idea Man — S.D.

To Rukhsana, who has great taste, and not just in cooking — Y.C.

Published in the United States 1999
by Dutton Children's Books,
a division of Penguin Putnam Books for Young Readers
345 Hudson Street
New York, New York 10014
www.penguinputnam.com

Produced by Somerville House Books Limited
3080 Yonge Street, Suite 5000, Toronto, Ontario, Canada M4N 3N1

Designed by Teri McMahon
Printed in China   First American Edition

2 4 6 8 1 0 9 7 5 3 1

ISBN 0-525-46255-4